THE BANK HEIST

Chronicles of Swordsfall

Brandon Dixon

Swordsfall Studios

ISBN-13: 9798634101224

Illustrations by T'umo Mere
Edited by Ianara Natividad
Cover Design by Taylor Ruddle
Written and Created by Brandon Dixon
Library of Congress Control Number: 2018675309
Printed in the United States of America
www.swordsfall.com

For everyone in my own Killer Krew, I wanted to bring a story. This was one of the first stories that popped in my head when I was crafting this eclectic Krew. It only seemed right to expand it into a proper short story. For my amazing and dedicated readers, I hope the image of the Krew on the open road sticks with you.

CONTENTS

THE ENTRY

Mustaf took a deep breath as he wiped the sweat from his brow. The damp ring around his shirt collar grew as the silver-haired woman stared daggers at him from the other side of his desk.

"As I said before, ma'am, we simply cannot store that here. I understand it's an, um, heirloom, but it's just not a good fit for us. We have a number of other services though—"

A shriek pierced the air, reverberating around the metallic walls of the lobby. Mustaf gasped as he sprang to his feet, papers gently drifting across his desk. His gaze darted back and forth, scanning the large room for the noise's source.

In the end, he didn't need to look long, as his eyes settled on the source of the distress. He pushed his glasses further up his face, taking a moment to process the scene.

A trio unlike anyone from the area had sauntered into the establishment's lobby. It was impossible not to see the hunk of man first. He had hands the size of melons with shoulders broad enough to carry a full-grown Abyssinian back to the stable. Mustaf could not tell exactly just how tall the man was, but his frame seemed to swallow the entire room.

In front of the behemoth stood two shorter women. One of them was noticeably shorter than the other—and almost comically so compared to the behemoth looming behind them— but had an aura that seemed to equalize their heights. The way she walked and smirked as customers stared with open mouths said it all. Her size was not a weakness. The group stuck out in the extravagantly decorated area, where the bank staff typically conducted business with well-to-do customers.

"What in the world was that horrible racket?" Mrs. Sumerline squawked, her voice cracking with annoyance. Her jewelry softly jangled as she turned her pointed gaze to the commotion.

Her protest fell silent, though Mustaf's focus stayed on the villainous-looking trio. His eyes darted over to the second woman. He awkwardly ruffled a stack of papers stowed next to him. She walked just in front of the other two, suggesting she was in charge. The gleam from the woman's shaved head highlighted her scars. The way her eyes seemed glued in his direction made his hands itch, and Mustaf started rubbing them.

His mind refused to accept the situation. Everyone who worked in commodities had been drilled to know this group. To fear them. This lithe, steel-eyed woman staring him down was no doubt Nubia—the head of the lawless consortium of pirates known as Heaven's Fall and the "King of the Divide." Her visage plastered the back areas, stock rooms, and break rooms of every trade good center, town hall, and financial institution on the Emerald Coast. He knew her face well from the flat dimensions of black and white ink, but live and in color? Well, seeing the sketches didn't do her scars justice. They failed to capture the swagger of someone who took what they wanted, at any cost.

Mustaf coughed reflexively, his mouth suddenly parched with his realization. Nubia's presence meant the enormous one must be La'Skrin, the muscle. Then, the shorter woman was Alara, the one-armed second-in-command of Heaven's Fall. Mustaf thought he remembered at least another member of Nubia's posse, the Master of Arms or some such. By now, his tongue had dried like sandpaper, driving home the point of their impending doom.

Mustaf slowly began to bend his knees, lowering himself as if to sit down, and momentarily forgot that he was already seated. He slowly reached out underneath his desk, feeling his way toward the recessed button.

Then something sharp and cold pressed against his throat. Mustaf's fingertips immediately stopped, just short of the alarm.

"Please do. The way you smell makes me wonder what color your blood is," a voice barely whispered, almost cooing, into his ear.

Now Mustaf knew where the fourth member was. His throat dried like the Great Vinyatian Desert, the knife at his neck squeezing out any moisture that remained. He whimpered, his lips quaking as he squeaked, "Killer Krew." The visage of the pirate lord filled his field of vision as she finally reached his desk. His dread only deepened when she peered at him with a sneer that could have set fire to steel.

"I hate that fucking name." Nubia tsked, twisting her head to look down on Mustaf. The scarred corners of her mouth pulled up, dismay clear on her face.

"I think it's fun, Captain!" The chirpiness from the voice behind Mustaf caught the sweat-drenched man off guard.

Nubia's eyes traveled from Mustaf to his captor, her scowl unchanged.

"Don't fucking encourage it, Nivan."

"Whaaaaaaaaaaaaat? But it's so fun. They even spell it with *two* Ks. It's catching on, Captain."

La'Skrin stood behind Nubia, silent and still like a statue. Only the movement of his eyes, scanning the room back and forth, conveyed the life behind them.

The smaller woman, Alara, ignored the conversation between the other two women and remained laser-focused on Mustaf. Her gaze differed from Nubia's death glare, but it had a similarly piercing strength. Mustaf, for the first time in as long as he could remember, felt trapped. Ironically, the silver and gold walls of the bank had always given him a sense of peace and solitude. It was a place of absolute safety where nothing, not even secrets, could escape—and for him, a place of freedom. Yet under this petite woman's gaze, Mustaf lost all sense of that safety. Her hazel eyes seemed to scan his mind, like a predator extracting all details of its prey.

3

After a few failed tugs at self-control, Mustaf broke away from the pirate's penetrating gaze. His eyes drifted over to the living, silent mountain behind her, then to the pirate lord. His despondent gaze eventually settled on the floor. However, the cool metal of the knife-edge posed to end his life at a moment's notice kept Mustaf's senses on high alert. He couldn't decide if death was imminent or not, his thoughts bouncing from one horrific outcome to the next.

The two cutthroats continued their squabble even as the front doors closed with sharp thuds. A few of the remaining customers had taken the odd moment to flee, the doors clanging loudly after them. Yet, neither of the pirates broke away from their argument. Didn't they need hostages? The way the criminals seemed unfazed only added to Mustaf's dread.

Nivan continued, "All I'm saying is there's nothing wrong with people knowing who we are, Captain. It makes their fear *that* much more real. You know that thing landies' eyes do when they're, like, *super* scared? Goes all wide and their pupils just go WHOOMP!"

The blade fell away from Mustaf's neck. He couldn't see her gesture, but given the sound, he imagined she had mimicked an explosion and illustrated with her hands. He quickly gulped, his sense of freedom coming back for a split moment.

Mustaf rubbed the sore point on his neck where the blade had pressed against him, swiping at a tiny stream of blood. As he gingerly rubbed around the cut, he noticed a shadow looming over him. He glanced up, right into the iron clad glare of Nubia. While Alara's gaze had been equal parts disarming and probative, the pirate lord's was completely predatorial. At that moment, Mustaf felt like a street rat in the gaze of a ravenous wolf with its jaws running over with saliva, ready for its next meal. He was just low hanging fruit, but on this day, he was a small and easy dinner.

"Looks like everyone else cleared out..." Nubia narrowed her eyes and sat down. She leaned forward, her petrifying gaze looking him over. "Mustaf. The sound of the door was another customer running in fright."

He blinked. Hearing his name spoken by the outlaw made his skin electric. His arms tingled, the hair on them standing up. Her voice rattled him the most. From the stories and the scars, Mustaf had intuitively expected the raspy growl of a killer—the hollow sound of someone with zero boundaries, fueled by moral depravity. When she spoke to him, however, she sounded slow and cold, patient even, like she was cooing at an animal before the final blow. Nubia had the quiet, slow speech of someone who controlled all the odds. With this display, she merely clued him into where he fit in this paradigm. Her voice conveyed a calm that somehow made her more fearsome.

"I... I don't know what you want. But the safe with Azurean chips is on a timer and takes an hour to open. I swear its true, and I can't override it either. Please, I swear. Don't kill me." Mustaf's voice broke again, his panic bubbling to the surface.

The pirate behind him—Nivan, as they called her—burst into a giggling fit. He stilled for a moment, horrified at the thought of what her laughter meant for him.

"See, Cap'n? Eveerrrrrytime," Nivan mused.

Nubia's mouth raised ever so slightly, the stern look almost breaking out into a smile. Her expression settled somewhere between mocking and self-assured. "Okay then, Mustaf. Take us into the private vault, then you can go back to your boring job." Nubia leaned forward and flicked his badge, punctuating her point.

"I'm afraid I don't know what you're talking about," Mustaf stammered, as his words wiped the bemusement from her face.

Nubia's intense scowl returned with a vengeance, and still leaning forward, she stared into his eyes. "Don't lie to me, Mussy." Her words came low, heavy with the prospect of violence.

"I'm—I'm not." He nervously wiped his palms on his pants. Nubia's attention had caused them to become slick again with sweat, the dew of fear.

"Alara?" The pirate lord leaned her head toward the smaller woman.

Mustaf glanced over at the one-armed pirate, only to see her piercing stare still aimed at him. He gulped silently, as he imagined what she had gleaned from the situation.

"Maybe he simply doesn't know about the ten square meter vault nestled in the back southwestern section of the bank. Concealed using the storefront nearby so it appears as if the bank isn't big enough for it. But that would entail knowing absolutely nothing about your job. Right?" Alara's wild buff of caramel-colored hair waved as she tilted her head.

Silence punched the air while Mustaf stared back, agape. He felt his armpits dampening again.

"But surely that's not the case, right? Mustaf Shorfront. Manager and facilitator of this said financial establishment." Alara smiled, punctuating the end of her statement.

Mustaf understood the pirates' intentions now. This hit wasn't just a smash and grab. They knew the bank's true purpose, and they wanted something specific from it.

Nubia grabbed him by the chin and tilted it in her direction. Her fingers gripped his face with a hold that didn't just guide, it demanded. "You heard her, Mussy. Care to lie again? Because I swore you were just begging for us to let you live." The smoothness of her voice sent shivers down his spine. How many times had she threatened someone this way?

"It's... it's complicated! I can't just let you back there. You don't understand who finances—" He stopped when the far too familiar knife returned to its perch at his throat.

"I'm thinking a light teal. You have just this hint of lilacs and sadness. Your blood just screams this cute little teal. I'm soooo close to finding out. We're so close, Mussy. Just one more lie. Mmmm?" Nivan cooed in his ear. The tickling sensation turned into a sting as she pressed the blade firmer into his neck, drawing another small stream of blood. "Awww, not quite that color. Hmm, but I'm sure if I get just a *little* deeper, we'll get the true color."

"Look. LOOK! Some of the areas—well, more *discerning* clientele use that private service. If you take something from there, it would be terrible, most terrible. Bad for *all* of us. You don't want to do that." Mustaf hoped he made his point clear, though it was hard to hear his own words over his heart's frantic beating.

"I'm growing bored of this, old man. Is that a yes or no?" Nubia spat out the words with sure intentions and little patience. She stood up, the light gleaming from her smooth head. The Killer Krew's leader wasn't tall, not by physical standards at least. She had some height over Alara, and the mammoth of a man didn't count for any comparisons. However, Nubia seemed to tower over Mustaf through her imposing presence alone. Something about the way she stood, her back straight and shoulders pointed forward, resembled a large, wild cat. She was like the living embodiment of a jaguar in the dead of the night.

"F... fine." Mustaf hung his head in defeat. The Vensota Family was the one group he thought he'd never cross, at least until this moment. With the most notorious corsair in the world standing in his bank—in front of his desk—well, his loyalties shifted. A feeling of utter powerlessness washed over him, reinforced by the patronizing pat on his head.

"I'm proud and disappointed in you at the same time," Nivan quipped.

The blade retreated from its threatening positioning at his neck, and Mustaf once again rubbed the tender spot of the cut.

"Well, lead the way, *Mussy*," Nubia commanded. She waved him forward, almost like a child. As Mustaf slowly stood and raised his hands to mark his surrender, Nubia rolled her eyes at him, apparently annoyed by the suggestion that he might have anything to hide. She already knew that they had his life in their hands.

When Mustaf turned around to proceed toward the bank vault, he finally saw the face of his morbidly gleeful captor. He just barely capped off the squeal that had burst from his mouth. Splashes of gold, black, and orange filled his vision, and Mustaf stumbled back a bit. Then, he realized he wasn't staring at a face, but at a mask. A colorful, ornate mask with the sidelines pulled out into the shape of a fox. Its bright and vibrant colors made it seem like it was floating over Nivan's face. Raven black hair hung to each side and over the top of part of the garish mask.

"Hiiii, Mussy. Like what you see?" Nivan chimed with a tilt of her head.

Mustaf couldn't see it, but he swore he could just hear her smile and stick her tongue out at him. He didn't know if he was supposed to respond. His mouth opened and then closed awkwardly like a fish out of water.

The room had fallen eerily still by now. The silence only punctuated his speechlessness. Mustaf's gaze darted around the room as he started to realize just how alone he was. While the Krew had grilled him for information, all the customers had already bolted.

Well, almost everyone.

Poor Mrs. Sumerline sat glued to her chair, eyes wide in terror. She hadn't moved an inch since the ordeal began. Mustaf might have worried she was dead if she didn't tremble like a leaf. In a way, the whole situation amazed Mustaf. He wasn't sure anyone on this planet could frighten the fiery senior. Unfortunately, Mustaf was still being held hostage. Then he felt a sharp shove from behind.

"I said. Lead. The. Way," Nubia uttered, her voice cold, low, and exact. Her tone alone relayed an underlying "or else."

The defeated man started walking toward the back area of the facility, away from the bank's main lobby. The general public knew they had some kind of backroom, but almost no one outside of the bank knew the details. Mustaf scratched his neck, where beads of sweat gathered around the collar of his shirt. He winced as his hand ran over the small wound that had opened up from his fussing. The man began to worry for more than just his life. What was worth more to a pirate than sellable goods? What could they be looking for in the vault?

"Pssh. Azurean chips," Nubia grumbled behind him, unimpressed as they passed by a pile. Almost as if she had read his thoughts.

"I... I truly don't know what's in the private reserve, so please don't hurt me if you don't find what you're looking for." Mustaf briefly glanced over his shoulder to see if the leader had heard.

Again, he was greeted with Nubia rolling her eyes and laughter from the masked woman.

"Private reserve? Is that what you call it? Really?" Nivan doubled over, her silky dark hair waving side to side. "HA!"

Maybe it was the blood loss, but Mustaf swore the mask just smirked. It was hard to imagine being more unnerved by her, and yet, it happened. They then reached the door to the back area. The small nine-key entry pad lit up as it sensed someone nearby. Mustaf reached out to punch in the oh so familiar numbers when Nubia grabbed him by the forearm.

"If you type in anything but the actual passcode, you're not going to like the outcome, Mussy." The captain's locked gazes with him like a predator eyeing a target. She released her grip.

With a slight twitch, he began entering the unlock combination, the keypad softly beeping to his frantic and anxious presses. Mustaf hesitated for a moment, thinking this could be a great opportunity to—

"Bad things happen if you put in the silent alarm code." The words slid from Nubia's mouth like a venomous snake.

He had suffered threats before; it came with the job. When you handled precious material, the clientele could get heated. But the way the Nubia uttered them? Well...

Mustaf input the correct code.

A loud click rang from the steel door before it swung open a bit. Mustaf grabbed the heavy door and began to pull back. However, he stopped as a meaty hand soared above him and drove it open with one smooth motion.

Mustaf looked up, eyes filled with pure awe, at La'Skrin—who had stayed so silent that he had almost forgotten about the colossal man entirely. "Tha... thanks," he squeaked.

La'Skrin nodded and motioned for him to continue. Beyond the heavy vault door was a simple hallway with carts and spare equipment stacked between several gated doors. Those gated entryways led to various stored goods like Azurean chips. Each door was made from a hardened alloy that could withstand any manner of physical attacks. Only the small window at the top of each one provided a glimpse at the contents. Mustaf slowed down, waiting for the Krew to start their looting.

"Keep walking, *friend*. Like I said, not here for this stuff." Nubia gave his back a sharp poke after she finished speaking.

Mustaf once again stood corrected, leading him to worry that much more about his fate. He continued down the hall to its end. A stack of broken carts lined against the wall, desperately in need of repair. The wall seemed like an apparent dead end, serving only to hold up the broken and disregarded equipment.

"I need you to close the vault door to access the private res —I mean, the back area. Please," Mustaf said, stumbling over his words.

He heard a muffled chuckle as Nivan responded to his change of words. La'Skrin pulled the door closed with ease. The way the man handled the couple hundred-pound door was impressive. Impressively intimidating. As the door clicked shut, the lights brightened, and a digital display lit up on the backside of the outer vault door, showing a standard 6-panel arrangement of security cameras. The screens showed the front entrance, the lobby, and where they stood in the inner vault.

The lobby looked empty, as it had been when they started walking into the vault. Mustaf, while not surprised, felt a tinge of disappointment. He had hoped that maybe someone had heard the disturbance and inquired, holding out for that last bit of luck before he had to commit to his actions. He sighed and resigned himself to the situation.

Mustaf walked up to the stacked carts used to transport goods from the safe to the floor. He reached over and twisted the handle on one, then grabbed the bottom cart and pulled. A secret panel opened next to carts. Similar to the one outside, it had a keypad on it. Mustaf entered some digits that the pad accepted with a peep. Another panel opened up behind it; this one had no keypad, but instead had a gaping circle. He then stuck his arm up to his elbow into the deep opening. The hair on the back of his neck stood up, as he sensed three sets of eyes on him.

"Remember what I said, Mussy," Nubia called behind him.

"It's not a trick! Just part of the security protocol, I swear." He threw up his free arm in surrender and felt a slight sting from the inserted arm. A loud series of metallic clicks rang out. With a hiss, a faint outline of a doorway began appearing on the wall next to Mustaf. Then, the section of the floor with the broken carts leaning against it swung out. The hidden door appeared heavily armored, over a foot thick itself.

Alara whistled behind him. "The folks around here really spare no expense when it comes to security."

"No kidding," Nubia agreed, "so what's the purpose of the arm insertion?"

Mustaf gingerly pulled his hand from the ominous security measure. "It's a biometric scanner. If you're not on the approved entry list, then the chapter tightens, trapping your arm and sending out an alarm."

"Whaaat? So it just... traps? It doesn't slice off your arm or anything?" Nivan practically leaped in front of him, her head tilting.

"Oh Ishvana, no. Just traps. Nothing so ghoulish as dismemberment," Mustaf replied.

"Well, that's disappointing."

Mustaf blinked, thinking to himself that the one with the mask was frightening in an entirely different way than the rest. Like a sadistic child, albeit probably deadlier.

With a faint buzz, the overhead lights slowly stirred to life in the bank's most inner hallway before them. Mustaf found himself hesitating as he stepped inside, a single, sensible shoe pausing over the threshold. Veins peaked along his forehead, and his jaw clenched, almost as if he was steeling himself. The grimly resolute man turned to see the fierce captain eyeballing him once again. Her gaze, without flinch or pause, locked onto him, and she stared at her catch with borderline disdain.

"I... I'm gonna do what you say, I'm not resisting—it's just, the people who own this, who funded this. They're very scary. On your level scary, and I mean that in the most respectful way possible. They run all matter of inventory through this area. And —and a lot of us have stayed *employed* by not asking questions."

Mustaf took a deep breath as he ended his appeal, his small burst of resolve draining from his body. He feared the worse as he waited for the pirate captain to answer.

Nubia gave the man a sharp and steady look down, like a parent staring into the eyes of their diminutive child.

"So?"

Silence washed over Mustaf for a few moments before he sputtered, "I—well, you—it's just—"

"No matter where you go, someone is always claiming they run something. I don't care anymore now than I did ten minutes ago. Vensota, Zencora, whatever." Nubia's joyless expression didn't change as she made her intentions clear.

The manager's brow creased further, creating waves across his forehead. His mouth opened again to speak.

"I. Don't. Fucking. Care." Her tone could have been a weapon. With each punctuated word, Nubia made it beyond clear that there wasn't anything to discuss.

Mustaf's eyes drifted over to the other three people. They all seemed to share the same level of disinterest. He stood there, a bit stunned. At first, he thought that maybe they didn't know who owned the vault, but now he could see that they just, well, didn't care.

The defeated manager nodded somberly and took the first steps into the secluded hallway. The smooth stone walls shimmered from the light bouncing off them. Each wall, the ceiling, and the floor lacked any grooves or indents, as if cut from one piece of fine stone. Luxurious marble painted the way to the bank's inner sanctum. The hallway was narrower than the one that had preceded it but wide enough for a mammoth man like La'Skrin to fit, albeit he had to duck his head a bit.

At the end of the marble-lined hallway, they reached a wide, open area. The center had a large sit-down table that could host two to four people. Lockers of various sizes lined the three sides of the room, all of them flush with the wall. They all featured the same intricate marble work of the vault's walls and preceding hallway. Some were only large enough for a single envelope, some had enough space for a canister, and the biggest ones looked like they could fit a human. Each of the units had two key locks.

Alara whistled as they entered the spacious area. "For a secret area, ya'll really know how to IM-PRESS." The petite woman ran her fingers along the black and white swirls on the marble of the nearest locker. "Anyone who puts this much effort into a room you only see a few times a year has a *lot* to hide."

Alara glanced around with a smile that could only spell one thing. Mischief. Nivan skipped along the perimeter of the room like a child on a stroll, running her fingers across the stone. Nubia had pulled a piece of paper from a pouch at her side and studied it with brief looks upward.

Nivan chirped, "Boss! When we can get to stealin'? I wanna see what all these rich, stuffy people are hiding. It's always the same, ya know? It's either naughty, nasty, or nice. Kind of like one of those mystery flavor candies they have at those booths on the Isle. You don't know what each flavor is, but you're *sure* it's that one flavor you'll like. So even if you eat one that's gross, you tell yourself it's ok, cause the next one? The next one you'll like. Then you find one you kinda like, but you're not sure if that's the perfect flavor, so you just kinda remember it for yourself and keep eating them. But then the bag is empty, and you have to decide which one you *actually* liked, but there's no more to eat so you're just going off of memory. I guess it's not exactly like mystery snacks, hmm maybe I'm just hungry..." She trailed off, turning around to see the entirety of the room staring at her. "If you ate a pack, you'd understand. Trust me."

Alara blankly stared at the masked pirate. La'Skrin had his face in his hand, and Mustaf was pretty sure the large man had squashed a laugh.

"The things you say, I will never fully understand," Alara dryly remarked.

"Ahhh thanks, Alara. I love you too!"

The mask didn't move, but again Mustaf swore he saw a smirk on it. Not too far from him, he heard a snicker escaping La'Skrin's mammoth hand, the giant failing to hide his humor at the moment.

Alara shook her head with a sigh and walked toward the captain, who had stopped to eye Nivan as well. "Captain?"

"Yea, I found what I'm looking for. Have at it everyone, before Nivan chews her way out of her mask." A sly smile tweaked at the corner of Nubia's mouth.

"This one is lime flavored," Nivan exclaimed from across the room.

Mustaf watched at the surrealness, or perhaps absurdity, of the situation. He could hardly tell at this point. Nubia's face, on the other hand, conveyed a mixture of "this is what I meant" and "oh... friend..." Either way, she walked toward the northern section of the private reserve, a piece of paper in hand. She glanced back and motioned La'Skrin to come with her.

Mustaf remained at a loss at what to do. Despite him being a hostage, the pirate crew had seemed to all but forgotten about him once they got to the vault. Was this the time to run? He looked back toward the exit and the long hallway he would have to cross. He didn't know how fast these corsairs were, but he knew he was not much of a runner. However, Mustaf had the motivation. Today, he'd find the speed.

He returned his eyes toward his captors to check one last time, only to let out a small squeak. Alara and her massive throng of curly, caramel hair stood only inches from him. Mustaf hadn't even heard her move or felt her approach.

"No, we haven't forgotten about you, honey. Sit tight and remember, we're *all* faster than you," she said while pinching his cheek, using a cutesy, mocking tone that cut the man to his core. The motivation he had a moment ago had deflated into a cold realization. He was at completely their mercy, and there wasn't much he could do.

That settled that.

Mustaf sulked over to one of the elegant tables and sat down.

"This one, please." Nubia's soft grumble was met by a thunderous crack that almost sent the manager's heart soaring out of his chest. La'Skrin had literally *shattered* the door to one of the personal vaults. With his bare hands.

Mustaf stared with a sense of sickening awe. The living behemoth had just squared up to the door and punched through—surgical, exact, and with a power beyond anything Mustaf could ever have imagined humanly possible.

"Ho—how? Those are all warded along with being made from three inches of reinforced ceramic steel. With a single punch?" The destitute hostage had doubted that the thieves could get into the vaults in the first place. The fact that one of them simply punched one open shattered *his* expectations.

Mustaf had heard plenty of corsairs, especially of the pirate group Heaven's Fall. They were a pseudo-urban legend, whispered about at meetings and work functions. But that was something people on the Grand Divide and the coastal areas of Garuda dealt with, not people like him. His bank was a hundred kilometers inland, far enough that he had never taken the information seriously. He only really learned enough to stay up-to-date with the office gossip.

No one answered Mustaf's question, so the man remained silent and simply watched. The stories that he heard? They were tame in comparison to the real pirate crew. As Mustaf stared helplessly from his spot, it looked like the captain of Heaven's Fall had finished her search.

Nubia pulled a box from beneath the broken pieces of the small vault door. She wiped the dust from the box and examined the exterior.

"That the one you looking for, Captain?" La'Skrin asked with a low but measured voice. To Mustaf, on first look the large pirate looked like brawn first, brains later, but the way he spoke hinted at something more.

The right side of Nubia's mouth pulled up into a happy smirk, the most positive expression on her face since the Killer Krew had appeared in the bank lobby. "I got exactly what I was looking for."

"Hey! Mind if I borrow that magical vault key you call a fist over here?" Alara shouted to La'Skrin.

The large man huffed and made his way toward his comrade.

"Hmmm. I *know* you can open up one of these," he said as he squared up with the door she had targeted for execution.

"Yea, but then I'd get all dusty, and ya just look so good doing it." She smiled wide and made a little heart symbol with her hands.

La'Skrin rolled his eyes at her. "You just don't feel like it," he retorted.

"Nope!"

He snickered before another thunderous crack rang out as he obliterated the vault door in an instant.

Alara smiled again and playfully punched his arm. "See, team-work. I'm sure the *extra* one could use you too."

La'Skrin shook his head and pointed his enormous thumb over his shoulder. "When it comes to getting into stuff, she doesn't need any help."

Mustaf, obviously eavesdropping, watched the two converse. Side by side, their size difference was almost comical in scale. The one-armed corsair stood only around four feet tall with about a foot of hair, and La'Skrin towered over her at almost seven feet. Mustaf's gaze also followed La'Skrin's thumb toward the masked pirate. His eyes widened in shock, a familiar and wanted friend at this point.

Nivan nustled in the southwestern corner of the vault with a collection of small piles scattered around her. She then skipped to a row of vaults, and the doors fell in two pieces just moments later.

Mustaf couldn't even see the weapon in hand because she moved faster than he could track. However, he was certain that Nivan had cut the vault doors in half with a single strike, and now, he watched as she caught the falling pieces and gingerly placed them in little piles. In the time it took for the large man to impressively destroy two vault doors, Nivan had done more, so much more.

Both Alara and La'Skrin had watched their crewmate work, and Alara nodded approvingly. "Well, that's one way to do it, I guess. Is she even grabbing anything or just cutting the doors?"

THE BANK HEIST

"Just cutting them," La'Skrin confirmed with a nod.

"I'm not sure if we should take her out more or less, to be honest," Nubia said as she joined in watching Nivan work, hovering over Alara but still dwarfed by La'Skrin.

"Less," they declared in unison.

Nivan paused, looking over her shoulder. "Huh? Why's everyone looking at me?"

"I'm wondering if you're gonna actually take anything or if you're just practicing or something," Nubia replied.

"Just looking for the right one, boss. Trying to find that special one that just really speaks to me, ya know?" Nivan's earnest tone carried on from beneath the painted mask.

Nubia nodded. "Yup, I definitely get it."

"Thanks, boss! I knew you'd get it—"

"You have thirty seconds left." Nubia turned and walked toward Mustaf, who sat transfixed by the scene. "We're leaving, Mussy," she said, roughly pushing the man to stand from the table.

Mustaf paused for a moment. He finally saw the weapon that Nivan had used to slice the vault doors in two. It seemed like an ordinary blade except for the green and yellow hues of the metal. She paused for a moment, and then she rapidly moved down the rows. She sliced at least three times at the impressive speed that Mustaf could barely see.

"She likes to cut stuff. Close your mouth, and get moving," Nubia ordered. She pushed him again, the box she procured snugly tucked under one arm.

"Oh! This one is calling my name," Nivan called out.

"Girl, you are *so* excessive," Alara chided, as Nivan came bounding with her new and ill-gotten treasure.

"Well someone has to make up for how boring you are," Nivan mused.

Alara, not one to be outgunned, retorted with some side-eye, "Everyone is boring compared to you."

Nivan put her finger to the painted lips of the mask. "Yea, you're probably right."

Mustaf was struck by the fact that, despite this being a rob-

ery, the gang of thieves seemed beyond relaxed. In fact, they
seemed to be enjoying themselves, as if they had no pressure to
finish their business and leave the building within a certain time.
He wasn't sure if this display stemmed from their expertise, fool-
ishness, or both. The fact that they've escaped capture for so long
suggested the former, but in this situation, he couldn't tell.

With Mustaf being pushed forward by Nubia to lead the way,
the group headed back the way they came. The masked corsair
showed off what she found to a completely uninterested Alara. As
they returned to the vault room, Mustaf noticed movement on
the security screen just slightly after Nubia did.

"Looks like you have a few extra guests in your bank, Mussy,"
the pirate lord said.

The six-panel monitor had been empty when they first entered the private reserve since all the customers already fled.
However, at least a dozen people in a mixture of armor and tactical gear now occupied the lobby.

"Oh no, oh no, oh no." Mustaf's heart started racing, as he rec-
ognized the equipment of the new entrants. His mouth began to
water, and bile crept up his throat. His lip quivered as he spoke,
"Those hired spears are from the Vensota family. Oh, Ishvana...
they must know I let you into the reserve. That's it! It's over.
I'm dead." Mustaf's knees wobbled, the pressure of the situation
draining his strength.

"Oh, Mussy. Of course they did. Like someone would put *that*
much effort into an ultra-secret, private vault and not have a secret alarm. How else do they make sure *you* don't try and rob
them?" Alara flicked a finger at his chest.

Mustaf's face dropped to a historical low, and he tugged at his
silver-tipped hair. It just now dawned on him that he had never
gone into the reserve without request. Of course they would have
a redundancy. And now, here they were. His eyes went wide as he
turned to his captors. He clasped his hands, his pupils full of earnest. "You have to tell them I didn't help you. You don't understand
who they are." He reached out to grab Nubia's arm but stopped
when her hawk-like gaze settled on him.

18

"You didn't hear anything my second-in-command said, did you? We know *exactly* who they are," Nubia said dismissively. She shoulder checked Mustaf out the way and moved toward the outer vault door. Alara followed wordlessly but with an equal look of determination and self-assuredness.

"Watch what's next, Mussy. It's gonna be FUN." Nivan flashed a peace sign at him and merrily followed her captain.

Mustaf speechlessly watched, completely unsure of what to do.

La'Skrin stopped to address the sniveling bank manager. The mammoth man laid a hand on Mustaf's shoulder, nearly engulfing it in his palm.

"Perhaps, Mustaf, this is a moment for you to reflect on who you choose for employment. A good employer would never hold you responsible for the actions of a highly trained crew of pirates. Consider thinking about how you truly want to live your life and the legacy you will leave. Is it worth working for someone who doesn't care? Just some food for thought." He slapped the smaller man on the back in solidarity, who stumbled a bit for the giant's benevolent gesture.

The bank manager felt like he was aging by the minute. He picked at the buttons of his baby blue jacket as the thieves made their way to the vault exit. He gently sat down on one of the genuine hauling carts. His hands grasped the cart's dull grey sides, rubbing the metallic surface as he contemplated the pirate's sermon.

Honestly, he always wanted to work in a library anyway. It was quieter. Much quieter.

THE LIFT

Nubia's eyes stayed glued to the security monitors. In place of the frightened customers, almost a dozen, stern-faced underlings occupied the lobby. These armed individuals had spread out around the room, covering both the exit to the bank and the vault entrance.

As the Krew came into view, a noise emanated from La'Skrin's right.

"It's the intruders. Vault entrance. Four confirmed." The shout originated from the other side of the vault door. Vensota's enforcers turned toward the now open vault and the pirate crew standing in its entryway. Just in time to see their comrade vanish with a sickening crack, as La'Skrin effortlessly shoved the vault door fully open with the flat of his palm. The door swung out with enough speed to pancake the man with a sickening crunch against the wall. The enforcers froze for a second as La'Skrin smiled slightly, cracking his fingers in the palm of his other hand.

At this point, the security monitors had deactivated once La'Skrin "opened" the vault. Nubia then turned her gaze back to the enforcers.

"Do you have any idea who you're fucking with? Who you just tried to fucking *rob*?" The sharp comment came from a figure who stepped forward. A well-built woman with her hair tightly pulled into a "just business" style glared at the Killer Krew, a wicked-looking spear in her hand. Like the rest, she was dressed from head to toe in tactical gear. Perhaps for anyone else, this display would have been intimidating. A sign of overwhelming force.

Nubia set down her plundered loot near the vault door. She stepped out from the partial shadows of the entryway, slowly approaching the apparent leader of this force until only a body length remained between them. A sneer slowly grew on the captain's face as she locked gazes with the hired spear, staring deeply at the mercenaries with narrowed eyes.

"Everyone keeps asking me that today. I'll tell you what," Nubia declared, leaning toward the leader a bit more. "When they finally unwire your jaw and you can speak again, make sure to tell the Vensotas *I* was here."

"I don't even know who you—" The spear-wielding spokesperson stopped mid-sentence as Nubia's knee rammed straight into their side, expelling all the air from her lungs with violent force. A perfect shot to the liver. Before the mercenary's liver could even bring them to their knees in crushing pain, Nubia connected a right hook straight to her exposed chin with a sickening crack.

The entire room paused for a second while the troops processed the quick disposal of their unit leader.

A defiant smirk adorned Nubia's face as she straightened her stance, chin raised. The trademark expression decorated her countless wanted posters and programs. In this circumstance, at this moment, the smirk fully and finally made sense. It was the smile of an apex predator in their natural habitat. However, for Nubia, she stood on top of the food chain regardless of her environment.

"Well, who's next?" the captain of Heaven's Fall yelled, still smirking. She pointed across the room, like a challenge for the rest of the enemy combatants.

Snapped back to their senses, a trio of enforcers rushed forward. Their spears whistled through the air with each thrust as they attempted to skewer the pirate. They only caught pure wind, however, since Nubia deftly spun and ducked past each of the strikes. She twisted and dodged another quick spear jab.

21

When the spearhead whizzed by, she trapped the shaft under her armpit. Nubia followed with a kick forward and spun her arm out, wrenching the spear from the enemy's grip, and with a flourish, it was hers now.

"Can I go yet, Alara? Caaaan I? Boss is having all the fun!" Nivan whined from beneath her fox-like mask.

Alara currently had her single arm stretched out, holding Nivan back like a broom barring a house cat. "You know better than that. Give her a minute. She's having fun." Alara had been at Nubia's side longer than anyone else. While many struggled to connect with the supreme commander of Heaven's Fall, Alara had an uncanny understanding of her.

Even Nivan knew better than to doubt the second-in-command when it came to matters with the captain, so she said nothing. She then crossed her arms and tapped her foot with all the grace of an angry teenager.

Nubia thrust twice with her newly acquired spear, marking the quick end of a mercenary as each hit connected. With a spin and a flourish, the weapon's blunt end caught another foe straight in the abdomen. They fell to the ground, retching from the liver shot. The third assailant stopped in place, shuffling their feet a bit as small beads of sweat gathered at their hairline. This merc had come to realize the harsh reality that they might have bitten off more than they could chew.

The enforcer glanced around at their comrades, who had started to fan out around the Krew but had yet to engage them. "Swarm them. There's only four!" one shouted. As if suddenly remembering their numbers, the Vensota enforcers surged forward, weapons at the ready.

Alara withdrew her arm from in front of Nivan. "*Now* you can go.".

"FINALLY!" Nivan shouted with child-like enthusiasm. She darted toward a group of three enemies, her hair flowing behind her like inky trails. Startled, one of the mercenaries quickly drew their sword as the flash of white and gold approached them. Less than a second later, the tip of the blade clattered to the floor with a metallic ping after Nivan had sliced through it like paper. There was only one master of blades in this room today, and it was time she showed them who.

"Shall we dance?" La'Skrin bowed formally to Alara. He then gestured toward the remaining forces looking in their direction.

"I thought you'd never ask," Alara responded with a wide smile, returning his bow. Two enforcers, swords drawn, came running toward her. She had gotten all too used to this part. Enemies would see that she had one arm and, well, *assume some shit*. But it always ended the same.

She dodged the downward swipe of the first blade by ducking under it. Using her momentum, she came up with a thunderous kick that sent the mercenary crashing into the desk beside them. Her curly afro swayed to the rhythm of her movements. Alara smiled sweetly at the other combatant when they hesitated after seeing the power of a single kick.

"Not so easy, am I?"

Before she could continue, an object came flying from the corner of her vision, smashing into the merc like a bolt from the blue. When the dust settled, Alara saw it was, well, another merc. She glanced over her shoulder and spotted La'Skrin holding one of the hired spears by the head, their whole face engulfed in the palm of his massive hand.

She scoffed at her colleague, "Really, 'Skrin? Really?"

"My bad... you want this one?" He pointed at the person futilely struggling in his vice-like grip, their cries muffled through La'Skrin's hand.

Alara blankly stared back at him for a moment. "It's not really something you just hand out."

"Fair. I'm just saying, I haven't knocked this one out yet, and I did take one of yours. So we can call it even, it's only fair." The merc started punching at La'Skrin's hand, who was completely unfazed.

"Yea, but it's the setup that matters. It's not the same when it's just handed to you. It's more about the moment, 'Skrin," Alara explained.

The large man paused. He tilted head slightly back, as he mentally chewed on the words. After a moment, La'Skrin nodded. "No, you right." He let go of the enforcer's face, letting them fall for a second before he struck with a dynamite punch. The sheer force sent the merc hurtling across the room, smashing through several desks and a chair.

At last, the room fell silent. Well, except for Nivan's humming. The masked crew member busied herself with searching through the pockets of the defeated enforcers, pulling out any knives and other weapons.

"Meh, these guys have poor taste. Nothing good on them *at all*. Cheap. Cheap. Ugly. Cheap. CHEAP!" Nivan stopped humming and released a dejected sigh. "Not even a good pocket knife. Boring."

La'Skrin approached and patted her softly on the head. "Next time, young one," he assured her.

"Next time!" Nivan eagerly agreed, the pep back in her step.

"Ya'll done bonding now? Or do you want to wait around for a second batch of them?" Nubia walked over to the rest of her crew, still playing with the spear she had used to dispatch her set of enemies.

"Oooh, can we?" Nivan clapped with excitement.

Nubia and Alara glanced at each other, saying nothing. Then, the pirate captain picked up her case from where she had dropped it just outside the inner vault and brushed off the bit of dust that had gathered on it. With her prize in hand, she made her way toward the front of the bank with Alara following her.

"Wait, so is that a no then? We're not gonna wait? Oh... I get it. You're just being rhetorical, huh, boss?"

The captain didn't respond as she stepped over the bodies strewn across the floor. One by one, the other pirates lined up behind their leader. They sauntered out the bank, their job complete. The sun had just started to come out from the midday cloud cover, and its rays now peered down on them—a right and cheerful match to the current mood of the Krew.

"Ooh, wait. Wait! Forgot two things, boss!" Nivan turned on her heel and bounced back into the bank.

"Three things if you count your mind!" Alara shouted back at her unpredictable comrade.

Unfazed, Nubia continued across the street, toward a light pink vehicle parked on the side of the road. Today had been a good day.

THE EXIT

Mustaf had watched in shock, slight horror, and a little amazement at the scene that unfolded. After seeing them crack open the vaults, he had no doubts the Killer Krew had earned their name for a reason, but watching the group take down a dozen highly-trained mercenaries was like a dream, or maybe a nightmare. Frankly, he didn't know how to feel about it, though he was glad it was over and that he had come out safe in the end.

Seeing how easily they had dispatched the Vensota enforcers, Mustaf felt fully justified in following the pirates' commands. Clearly, he had no other choice since there was definitely no way he could have run from them. Not a chance. After watching that battle, he thought himself supremely foolish for even entertaining the notion. Mustaf fixed his tie while he gathered his wits about himself. He was the bank manager after all, and though he had survived a great emergency, he still had a job to do. The mess outside, not to mention his own situation, wouldn't straighten itself.

Mustaf walked up to one of the gated doors to their Azurean chip stockpile. He didn't know what they took from the private reserve since the bank didn't keep specific records. The way Mustaf looked at it, the loss wasn't his responsibility. His job was to secure the bank's funds, and that he had done. He smiled to himself for the first time that morning.

"Everything will be alr—"

"Hey, Mussy!"

Mustaf squealed and jumped. He nearly tumbled to the ground before grabbing onto the gate's window bars for stability. His heart sunk like a rock as the now all too familiar masked face of Nivan stared back at him.

"I forgot two things! One of them you won't like, but you'll thank me later. The other one, well, you *really* won't like. But I will!"

The weary man stared back at her and sighed. "I quit."

***

Alara started the engine. Their car began to lift, the wheels retracting into the wheel well of the vehicle. The pink convertible swayed side to side for a moment before the balancer kicked in, stabilizing the car to offset La'Skrin's large mass in the back.

Nubia settled in the passenger seat, staring intently at the soft brown box in her lap—the single thing she had taken from the private reserve. Ornate lines and beautiful symbols covered its surface. Some of the inscriptions even looked like runes.

"So Nu', what's in the box? Are those sigil runes on it?" Alara questioned, eyeing the wooden box that they had traveled all this way to get. "I can only imagine what a power-mad family like the Vensotas had stored in there."

"Something I've been after for a long time now," Nubia replied in a low voice. Her fingers traced the delicate etching on the box.

The car shook and swayed for a second when Nivan leaped into the backseat. The sack she carried struck La'Skrin in the chest before it fell on his lap.

"Really?" he said, raising an eyebrow at her.

"Oh Divide, what did you go back in there for this time, Nivan?" Alara chided, as she turned around to see what the Master of Arms had gotten. The sack in La'Skrin's lap had opened as it fell in his lap, some of the contents spilling to the car floor.

Azurean chips.

"Really?" Alara asked in the same tone as La'Skrin, shaking her head at Nivan.

"Whaat? It *is* a bank after all. What would they think of the Killer Krew if we didn't, ya know? Rob the place?" Nivan did her best impression of a teacher, wagging her finger at them.

"Hate that name still," Nubia quipped from the front seat. Finally, she undid the front latch on the box.

"Oh, oh! Are we gonna finally see what we went to all this trouble for?" Nivan clapped her hands and leaned forward to get a view of the box. Even La'Skrin peered over the top of the seat with curiosity.

"Only five were ever made. Each given to the head of a nation. Hawklore's is in Hawken's personal vault at Eagle Eye Tower. Vinyata's was destroyed at the Eastern Node. Grimnest's is lost and who knows where. King Matan has Ramnos's. And Garuda's? Well, theirs... was stolen by the Vensota clan," the captain narrated while slowly lifting the lid. Nubia pulled out the single object that had laid so lovingly on the blue satin that lined the case's insides.

"And now, its mine," Nubia said. She unfolded the vaunted object and put it on her face. "The Ultra Special Edition, *King 5*s." Nubia smiled wide from behind the black-rimmed sunglasses, its frames glittering with hints of gold.

Alara laughed and put the car in gear. "Every king needs a pair after all."

"That's what I'm saying," Nubia confirmed with a nod.

La'Skrin chuckled. He sat back and gathered the faint blue square chips from his lap and placed them back into the bag. "You said you had two things to do. This is one. What was the other one, Nivan?" he inquired to his backseat partner as the car started accelerated down the road. He couldn't see her smile, but with the whimsical sound she made, La'Skrin knew it was something mischievous.

A trio of Celestial Shields cautiously entered the bank's front lobby, spears drawn at the ready.

"We are the Celestial Shields of the Eternal Flames. We have received reports of a robbery. If you are a combatant, surrender now and this will end peacefully." The Shield's words echoed throughout the empty lobby. One of them pointed toward the back of the room.

They saw the signs of a fight: desks flipped over or completely smashed; blood splatters all around; and yet, not a single body to be found. The elite protectors wordlessly looked at each other while slowly surveying the scene. Still, they remained on alert for any potential threats for this strange situation.

"That looks like the Vault door. It's open," one of them stated.

The trio slightly fanned out and began approaching the vault door, which had been left just several inches open. One of Celestial Shields saw movement through the crack between the door and frame.

"Looks like someone is in there."

One of them slowly opened the vault, struggling a bit under its weight as the other two readied their spears. As the door opened further, muffled sounds drifted out. With one more push, the team could use the opening to enter. One of the Shields whistled when they saw the destruction in front of them. The two gated doors on each side of the vault hallway had all been destroyed. One of them almost looked like someone had cut it open. Azurean chips littered the floor in what seemed like a hasty robbery.

In the middle of the mess, an older man with disheveled salt and pepper hair sat with his hands and ankles bound. A crudely-tied gag around his mouth muffled his voice. As the Shields approached the struggling man, they saw a message written on his forehead. The marker used for it laid on the floor next to him.

One of Shields chuckled and pointed it out to the others.

"Well, I guess we know who was responsible now," they mused with a barely covered snicker.

Another one removed the gag from the bank manager's mouth. "You're going to be okay, sir. We're here, and further help is on the way... do you know who did this?"

Mustaf's nose flared with anger, saliva returning to his mouth.

"Who do you think?" Mustaf angrily spat while pointing to his forehead.

There in marker, a simple message was elaborately scrawled.

"Thanks for the fun!
Love, The Killer Krew"

GLOSSARY OF
MAJOR TERMS

Azurean Chips – A small plastic chip that holds a set amount of Azurean. A popular form of currency in much of Garuda.

Beneath It All – A separation pocket dimension where Xavian is sealed

Ether – The name for the energy that powers all life.

Emerald Coast – A strip of coast where the southwestern corner of Garuda meets the the Grand Divide.

Garuda – The largest nation in the Northern Hemisphere. Home to The Divinity and controlled by The Divine Order of the Phoenix

Grand Divide, The – The name of the grand ocean that encircles all of Tikor.

Etherforce – The name for the natural occurring flow of Ether

Heaven's Fall – The largest legion of pirates in all of Tikor.

Ilun Valley – The most populace part of Garuda with a number of cities, towns and villages nested in its various caverns, cliffs and valleys.

Ishvana – An ancient creation god that is responsible for creating Tikor and much of its life. Sacrificed herself to seal Xavian.

Hekan - The name of magic in Tikor

Raksha – Ravenous monsters created by Xavian, sealed in Beneath It All

The Divinity – The general name for all the deities of Garuda. Also, the specific name for a group of the oldest and most revered of Garuda's deities.

Vinyata – The largest nation in the Southern Hemisphere. Home to The Four Pillars and controlled by The Republic of Vinyata.

Xavian – An ancient corruption god responsible for the corruption of the Elementals. Sealed away in Beneath It all.

ABOUT THE AUTHOR

Brandon Dixon

Brandon lives in the Portland area of Oregon with his other half, Ashley. When he's not obsessed with Swordsfall, he works fruitlessly on completing his burgeoning Steam game library.

Sign up for Swordsfall's newsletter at: https://www.swordsfall.com/newsletter-signup/

Connect with Swordsfall:
WEBSITE: swordsfall.com
PATREON: patreon.com/swordsfall
TWITTER: twitter.com/swordsfall1
FACEBOOK: facebook.com/swordsfallrpg
INSTAGRAM: instagram.com/swordsfallrpg

BOOKS BY THIS AUTHOR

Volume 1: Tikor, The Beginning | A Swordsfall Lore Book

Tikor is a world where deities and spirits are as real as the nature that surrounds them.

Since the earliest writings of mankind, the gods have been there with them.

Swordsfall isn't just a story, it's a world. It's a dive into pre-colonial Africa for all the rich lore you've never heard of.

It's an exploration into a world where the majority of the faces are dark, yet isn't constrained to one corner.

It's a world where women hold power equal to men and the merit of one's soul is what propels them through life. It's a world where spirits aren't to be feared, they are to be embraced. In a time where we know that representation matters, this project is an effort to add to that spirit in the way I know best.

Enter the world of Tikor, a world of Afropunk. A world that's never been seen before.

Four Stages: A Swordsfall Lore Book

A Short Story set within the Swordsfall Universe

A Spirit Medium from an elite division known as The Eyes of Garuda was commissioned to help in the investigation of a grisly quadruple homicide. The investigators assigned were baffled by the case. What they uncovered during the Mediums vision would change everything.

This vision would give the first glimpse into Xavian's Touch, a deadly mixture of curse and disease that links the victim to The Withering King himself, Xavian.

The following is a re-telling of what the Medium saw that fateful day.

The Four Stages of Xavian's Touch
Stage 1 - Infection

Stage 2 - Host Preparation

Stage 3 - Mental Degradation

Stage 4 – The Invitation

The Summit Of Kings, Battle For The Supreme Jalen: A Swordsfall Rpg Adventure

The Summit of Kings is a 2 – 4 player one-shot set in the Swordsfall universe. It can be played in several different ways. You can play it as a fun one-shot with your group, or an amusing detour for the Jalen in your Swordsfall group. Or, with a bit of homebrewing, an adventure in your system of choice. Either way, the goal is to have a unique experience of a classic rap battle of your table.

The Summit Of Kings

Once a year there is a special, one of a kind tournament held on the beautiful coast of The Isle. The Summit of Kings. A yearly battle where the top Jalens from around the world are invited to find out who is the best in straight oratorial combat. The only way to get into the Summit is through a special invite. Regardless of how well you place at The Summit, just the act of receiving an invite is considered a prestigious honor. The worldwide Jalen organization, The Sixteen, keep track of the millions of wordsages around Tikor. When the list goes out, the people listen. So, after spending months powering through the tales, speeches, and recordings of current Jalens, the Hot List is formed. The tournament set.

Over 10,000 people flock to the private beach, Boogie Cove, and the town that surrounds it, South Onyx, to witness the awesome battle. The partially secluded vista is the perfect backdrop for the lyrical battle. Owned by the reclusive Grandmaster Jalen, Flayshe, it serves as a gorgeous backdrop for the lyrical tournament.

Who Will Be Crowned The Wordsmith?

The rules are simple. One on One, Jalen vs Jalen, Winner Takes All. Each Jalen takes there turn delivering the most crowd thrilling rap possible while the other patiently watches, careful to maintain a neutral face. They each vie for the roar of the crowd and the growing look of defeat on their foes face. Each summit battle lasts for three rounds with the winner being the best out of two.

Includes Character Sheets

Summit of Kings comes with it's own character sheets. And not just any, but the fancy kind. You can print them as normal or use your favorite PDF software to enter in the values on the sheet itself.

Printable (Black & White and Color)

Fillable (Black & White and Color)

Made in the USA
Columbia, SC
20 March 2022